20,000 LEAGUES UNDER THE SEA

ORIGINAL BY JULES VERNE

RETOLD BY PAULINE FRANCIS

First published in this edition in 2010

Cover design and illustration by Emil Dacanay, D.R. Ink
Inside illustrations by Steve Angel

British Library Cataloguing in Publication data
A cataloguing record for this book is available from the British Library.

ISBN 978-93-5275-582-0

Published by Scholastic India Pvt. Ltd. under license from
Readzone Book Limited, February 2019, March 2021

This reprint edition : May 2026
Printed at Sterling Graphics Pvt. Ltd., Manesar

20,000 LEAGUES UNDER THE SEA

CHAPTER One *Monster at Sea* 5

CHAPTER Two *A Strange Whale* 10

CHAPTER Three *The Nautilus* 14

CHAPTER Four *A Walk under Water* 18

CHAPTER Five *Buried at Sea* 24

CHAPTER Six *Saving Captain Nemo* 27

CHAPTER Seven *The Arabian Tunnel* 31

CHAPTER Eight *Atlantis* 34

CHAPTER Nine *The South Pole* 38

CHAPTER Ten *Escaping the Whirlwind* 42

Introduction

Jules Verne was born in northern France in 1828. He went to study law in Paris, as his father had done. But as well as studying, he began to do what he really wanted – to write.

Jules Verne wrote several plays and some of them were performed on the Paris stage. In 1857, he married a widow with two young sons. He continued to work and write because he had a family to support.

In 1862, Jules Verne wrote his first travel adventure, *Five Weeks in a Balloon.* It soon became very popular. From then on, Verne wrote for the same publisher, called Hetzel. In 1869, *Twenty Thousand Leagues Under the Sea* was published. This book tells the story of a scientist who is trying to rid the ocean of a sea monster. Instead, he becomes a prisoner of Captain Nemo and is forced to travel around the world – under the sea. When this story was written, real scientists were still trying to design a submarine that could stay under water for a long time.

Jules Verne wrote over sixty more novels before his death in 1905. The best-known of these are *Journey to the Centre of the Earth* (1864) and *Around the World in Eighty Days* (1873).

Chapter One

Monster at Sea

I was in New York in the summer of 1867. I had just finished a scientific expedition and was waiting to sail back to France where I worked at the Museum of Paris. One morning, this newspaper article caught my eye:

2nd July, 1867, New York Herald

SEA MONSTER STRIKES AGAIN!

A sea monster has attacked two ships in the Pacific Ocean. It made holes in the ships with its sharp teeth, although not badly enough to sink them.

It is thought to be the same creature that was seen several times last year. It has been described as "bigger than a whale" and about two hundred feet long. Sometimes it shines brightly.

What is this creature that lurks beneath the waves? We shall soon find out. The "Abraham Lincoln" has been ready for some time to set sail. It is a high-speed, ice-breaking ship that will soon hunt it down.

"There are only two explanations for what has happened,"

I thought. "It is either a very powerful ship that travels under the sea – but such an engine has not been invented yet – or a very powerful sea creature."

A short time later, this letter arrived at my hotel:

Dear Monsieur Aronnax

If you wish to join the expedition of the Abraham Lincoln *to represent France, the Captain has reserved a cabin for you.*

Yours,
Secretary of the Navy.

I did not hesitate. "Conseil!" I called to my manservant. "Start packing. We are going to rid the sea of a monster! It will be a glorious journey, but a dangerous one. It is the sort of journey from which people don't always come back."

"Whatever pleases Monsieur," Conseil replied calmly.

By eight o'clock that evening, we were sailing into the dark waters of the Atlantic Ocean. The ship had all the equipment needed for capturing the giant sea creature – harpoons, cannons and other guns. But best of all, she carried Ned Land, a man with the reputation of being one of the best harpooners around.

Ned Land was about forty years old, a Canadian from Quebec, a town that still belonged to France. He looked serious and did not speak very much. He became angry very easily if somebody annoyed him. He took a liking to me because I was French.

"I do not believe in this sea monster," he told me.

"But you are a whaler," I replied. "You ought to accept the idea of an enormous sea mammal."

"That is exactly why I don't believe it," he replied. "I have hunted and harpooned many in my time and none of them were powerful enough to have holed an iron ship. I suppose it *could* be a giant octopus. Have you thought of that?"

"That is even less likely, Ned," I replied. "Its flesh is too soft, even if it were five hundred feet long."

On the 27th of July, we entered the Pacific Ocean. At last we were in the area where the monster had last been seen. We were all excited and could not eat or sleep. But day after day, we saw nothing. The crew became angry and felt they were wasting their time.

At the beginning of November, our ship was less than two hundred miles from the coast of Japan. Night was falling and the sea was calm. I was with Conseil on deck when Ned's voice rang out. "Ahoy! There it is at last!" he shouted. "Right behind us!"

"Stop the engines," the captain called.

In the distance, the sea seemed to be lit from below, as if the monster was giving off a bright light. Then the light began to move towards us. Our ship reversed and moved away, but the creature came towards us at a speed twice our own. It circled us, glowing brightly. Then it moved away, leaving a trail of light. Suddenly it rushed at us again, stopping only a few feet from us. Then it vanished.

"Let us wait for daylight," the captain said. "Then we can do the attacking."

We could hear the creature all night – the thrashing of its tail, the sound of air being sucked into its lungs and the noise of water being blown out. When daylight came, the creature's brilliant light went out and a long, black body emerged a yard above the water. Its seemed to be about two hundred and fifty feet in length and it shot water high into the air.

"Full steam ahead!" the captain shouted.

A cheer from the crew filled the air as we went forward to do battle. But we could not catch up with the creature. What a chase! I trembled with excitement every time it allowed us to come closer. Ned Land sat at the bow, harpoon ready in his hand. The creature teased us all day. We never caught it, however fast we went – and it circled around us all the time.

"Prepare to fire the cannon!" the captain cried at eight o'clock that evening.

The third cannon ball hit its target, but it bounced off the creature's skin. So the chase began again. We travelled about three hundred miles that first day, until darkness fell. Then the brilliant light appeared about three miles away. It seemed to be still and we sailed silently towards it. Suddenly, the light went out and two enormous jets of water hit the ship's deck. There was a terrible jolt and I lost my balance.

I fell over the rail and into the sea.

Chapter Two

A Strange Whale

I was dragged about twenty feet below the waves, but two strong kicks brought me back to the surface. I watched the *Abraham Lincoln* disappear into the darkness.

"Help! Help!" I cried in desperation.

My mouth filled with water and I felt myself suffocating. Then strong hands pulled me up. It was Conseil.

"Were you flung overboard, too?" I asked him, gasping for breath.

"Not at all, Monsieur," he replied. "I work for Monsieur, so I had to follow him."

"Where is the ship?" I cried.

"Monsieur must forget about it," he replied. "Its propeller and rudder are broken. It cannot turn back for us now."

We swam side by side, but I knew that the situation was desperate. A few hours later, we bumped into something hard. I was so weak that I could not hold on. Then I felt somebody pulling me up and I fainted. When I opened my eyes again, I saw Ned Land in front of me.

"This is a monster made of metal!" he cried.

I realised then that we were sitting right on top of the sea creature we had been hunting. Its back was smooth and shiny and it made a metallic sound when I tapped it.

"It must have been made by man!" I said. "And there must be an engine because it can move so quickly."

"I have been here for three hours," Ned replied, "and I have seen no sign of life. It hasn't even moved."

As he spoke, we heard a bubbling sound at the end of the strange machine and it began to sink slowly into the sea. Ned stood up and began to kick against the metal, shouting at the top of his voice. Almost at once, the machine stopped diving and a hatch opened. Eight men wearing masks appeared and, without a sound, they pulled us inside their machine. The hatch closed and we were in total darkness. The men pushed

us into a room and locked the door. Ned kicked against it, shouting angrily again.

"Keep calm, Ned," I said, "and do not get us into trouble. Let us try and find out where we are first!"

After half an hour, a brilliant glare lit our prison, like the bright light we had seen at sea. Soon afterwards, two men entered, speaking to each other in a language I did not recognise. We told them our story in French, English, Latin and German, but they did not understand a word. However, they brought us good food and clean water, after which we all fell into a deep sleep. When we woke up, the machine was so silent that I was afraid.

"Perhaps we are at the bottom of the sea," I thought, trembling.

The door opened at last, but Ned Land threw himself like a wild beast at the man who came in.

"Stop, Master Land!" a voice said in French. "My name is Captain Nemo, the captain of this ship. Please listen to me! I understood what you were saying yesterday, but I did not want to speak. I wanted to find out more about you first. Why have you chased me across the ocean?"

"Monsieur," I replied, "you must know of all the problems you have caused by damaging ships. We thought there was a dangerous monster in the sea."

"I no longer live in the world," he said, his eyes flashing with anger, "and I no longer have to obey any of its rules.

But I do pity you. And for that reason, I shall allow you to stay on one condition – there may be things I do not want you to see and you will have to stay in your cabins whenever I give the order."

"Are you saying that we are prisoners?" I asked.

"Yes," he replied. "You have found out my secret. I do not want the world to hear about it." He stared straight at us.

"I could throw you to the bottom of the sea," he said at last.

Chapter Three

The Nautilus

Captain Nemo invited me to eat with him. I soon realised that it was because I was the only scientist among us and he wanted talk about the *Nautilus*. I accepted his invitation eagerly.

"I love the sea," he told me. "On the surface, men are still killing one another. But down here, in the *Nautilus*, I am free to live as I wish!"

His ship was magnificent. The library contained twelve thousand books and many fine paintings. He had a wonderful collection of sea creatures and shells, all classified – and the best collection of pearls I had ever seen.

"Tell me more about the *Nautilus*," I said, when we sat down in his cabin to talk. "How do you manage to make so much electricity?"

"My electricity is not the one you use on land," he replied. "I extract the sodium from the seawater and use that in my batteries. I owe everything to the sea – it produces electricity to give us heat, light and movement."

"What about air?" I asked. "You can't make that."

"I can float to the surface whenever I choose," he replied. "And I store extra air in huge tanks."

"Captain Nemo," I said. "I have already seen your speed and skill in outrunning our ship. How do you steer the *Nautilus*? And how can you go so far below the water without breaking up?"

"It has two hulls," he explained. "One is inside the other. To go below the sea, I fill her tanks with water so that we sink. To rise, they are emptied. As for steering, that is simple. The *Nautilus* has fins, like a fish. And the steering platform has a panel made of special glass that does not break under water. As you have already seen, there is a powerful beam that can light up the water for half a mile."

"So how did you collide with the *Abraham Lincoln*?" I asked.

"I did not," he replied. "It was attacking me and I had to defend myself. I damaged her steering so that she could not turn back to attack me again."

Captain Nemo reached out and pressed an electric bell three times. "Now the tanks will empty," he said. "We are going to rise to the surface. I have to take our bearings from the position of the sun before we leave."

A few minutes later, he led me up a staircase, through an open hatch and out onto a platform, which rose about three feet above the sea. I looked around me in amazement. In the middle of the platform was a dinghy inside its own compartment, and at either end were two cages, partly made of glass. One was for the steersman, the other held the powerful electric searchlight. The ship was shaped like a cigar, and its iron plates overlapped to make it strong.

The sea was very beautiful and the sky was clear. There was nothing in sight, not even an island. There was nothing but a vast and deserted sea. When Captain Nemo had taken our bearings, we went down below once more into the saloon.

"Today is the eighth of November," he said, "and it is midday. Now we shall begin our voyage of exploration under the sea." He handed me a set of sea charts. "You may follow my route, Professor Aronnax, if you wish."

Captain Nemo bowed and left me to my thoughts. I stayed alone for an hour examining the charts, until Ned and

Conseil came to find me.

"Where are we?" they asked.

"More than one hundred and sixty feet below the sea," I told them.

"If Monsieur says so, then it must be true," Conseil replied.

Ned started to question me and I told him everything I knew. "The *Nautilus* is an amazing piece of engineering," I said. I stared hard at him. "You must give up any hope of escaping."

As I spoke, the lights went out.

"We are all going to die!" Ned cried.

Chapter Four

A Walk Under Water

We did not speak or move. Suddenly we heard a noise as if something was being pulled back and lights appeared on both sides of the saloon. We could see water all around us.

"Only two plates of glass separates us from death!" I gasped.

We leaned against the windows, filled with amazement.

"How strange!" Ned muttered. And for a moment, he forgot his anger and his need to escape.

For two hours, we watched the sea creatures around us. They leapt and splashed, each one faster and more graceful than the last. I had never seen them before in their natural setting. Then, suddenly, the panels closed again and all that beauty vanished.

We did not see Captain Nemo for a week. Then, on the eighth day, this note appeared in my cabin:

Professor Aronnax
The ***Nautilus***
16th November, 1867

Captain Nemo invites you and your friends to visit the forests of the Island of Crespo tomorrow morning.

"So we must be near land," I said.

"Good!" Ned cried. "I can hunt fresh meat at last."

But Ned was disappointed when we went to meet Captain Nemo.

"My island is under the sea," he explained to us.

"Then I shall not come with you," Ned replied.

"The captain must be mad!" I thought. "Divers have to stay close to their ships so that air can be pumped into their helmets."

Captain Nemo noticed the look of surprise on my face. "I have found a way to carry air on our backs," he explained. "It will last for ten hours. And I have special suits and helmets to protect us. Now it is time to put them on."

"We are thirty feet under water," I said. "How do we get outside?"

When we were ready, Captain Nemo led us into a small room. A door closed behind us and I felt the water rising over me. As soon as the room was full, a second door opened and, minutes later, our feet were touching the bottom of the ocean.

Words are not enough to describe our walk that day. The light that filtered down to us was amazingly strong and it was reflected in the flowers, rocks and shells. It was a

beautiful sight and a feast of colour.

The Forest of Crespo was full of large plants like trees, all growing straight towards the surface. They did not have any roots, but took their food from the water. They had brightly coloured blades instead of leaves.

We were very tired as we made our way back to the *Nautilus*. I was on the point of collapse when we saw its lights gleaming ahead. Suddenly, Captain Nemo turned round and pushed me to the ground. I raised my head to look and my blood froze in my veins. I was staring at the terrible jaws of two sharks. Fortunately, they had not seen us. We escaped death by a miracle. Half an hour later, guided by the beam of light, we were safely on board the Nautilus.

During the days and weeks that followed, I hardly saw Captain Nemo, but one of the crew marked the ship's course on the charts, so that I always knew where we were. The glass panels of the room were kept open and we never tired of seeing the beauty of the underwater world.

By the beginning of January, I calculated that we had travelled 11,340 miles, or 5,250 leagues, since we had left Japan. Now we were cruising through the dangerous waters of the Coral Sea, northeast of Australia. To reach the Indian Ocean, we had to travel through one of the most dangerous stretches of water in the world – the Torres Strait.

We entered the narrow passage where the water foamed and seethed around us, but we seemed to slip through as if by magic – until we came to a part known as the Evil Channel. There the *Nautilus* struck a coral reef off the coast of an island. She was so well built that she suffered no damage.

"If we cannot refloat, you may have to live on land again," I said to Captain Nemo. "The tides in the Pacific are not very strong."

Captain Nemo gave me a curious look. "In five days time there will be a full moon," he said. "I expect the water to rise high enough to float us again. We shall leave at exactly 2.35."

Ned Land became impatient. He wanted to go outside and take a look at the island. To our surprise, Captain Nemo agreed. He knew that it was better to be a prisoner on board his ship than to be at the mercy of wild animals and people who lived there. We set sail in the dinghy armed with rifles. It was exciting to set foot on land again after two months at sea! Ned could not contain his joy at being free at last, and being able to hunt for meat. We went back the following day, too, and explored until darkness began to fall.

"What would you think," Ned asked, "if I suggested that we never go back to the *Nautilus*?"

As he spoke, a stone fell amongst us, followed quickly by another. We jumped to our feet and raised our rifles as a group of Papuans with bows and arrows appeared at the edge of the forest. We managed to reach the boat safely, but as we pushed out to sea, there were more than a hundred men screaming and shouting at the water's edge. By the time we reached the *Nautilus*, the shore was silent and I went back to my cabin to sleep.

The next day, as the morning mist cleared, I saw the Papuans again. They were nearly all armed with bows and arrows and slings full of stones. They prowled around the ship during that low tide, but they did not cause any trouble. As we waited for the water to rise, Ned and I went outside to fish and look for interesting shells. We did not notice that about twenty canoes had surrounded the ship until arrows struck its side.

Then we ran back inside and Captain Nemo closed the

hatches immediately.

I decided to go to bed, but I slept badly. I could hear the footsteps and shouts of the Papuans walking up and down above me.

"How will we be able to take in fresh air before we leave tomorrow?" I asked myself. "They will kill us if we open the hatches."

Chapter Five

Buried at Sea

I was anxious the whole of the next morning. I went to the saloon to look at the clock. It was half-past two.

"If the *Nautilus* does not move soon, we shall be stuck here for months," I thought.

Five minutes later, Captain Nemo came into the saloon.

"We are going to take in air," he said. "I have given orders for the hatches to be opened."

"What about the Papuans?" I asked. "They will invade the ship."

"It is not easy to enter the hatches, even when they are open, Monsieur Aronnax," he replied. "Come and see."

I went with him. The hatches opened outwards and we saw fierce-looking faces peering down at us. One man put his hand on the staircase to climb down. He was thrown backwards and, with a terrible scream, he ran away. Ned ran up the stairs and grabbed the rail. He, too, was thrown back.

"I've been struck by lightning!" he cried.

"The rail is connected to the ship's electricity," I shouted.

At that moment, at exactly 2.40, the *Nautilus* was lifted from her coral bed by the rising tide. She picked up speed and soon left the Torres Strait far behind. I was full of admiration for Captain Nemo and the incredible ship he had designed.

On the 18th January, we entered rough seas. Captain Nemo stood looking through his telescope and seemed to be arguing with one of his men. I felt the speed of the ship increase. I took out my telescope to look at the horizon. But as soon as I put it to my eyes, Captain Nemo snatched it from me.

"I must ask you to remember what I said when you first came aboard," he said. "Please stay in your cabins until I decide to let you out again."

A few minutes later, we were locked in the cell where we had spent our first night. As soon as we had eaten, we all began to fall asleep and our breathing grew weaker. "Somebody has put sleeping pills into our food," I whispered to myself. I felt very cold and I could hardly move. Sleep overcame me. To my surprise, I woke up in my own cabin.

Nobody knew what had happened. The *Nautilus* seemed as quiet and mysterious as ever. At about two o'clock in the afternoon, Captain Nemo came to see me.

"Are you a doctor, Professor Aronnax?" he asked.

"Yes," I replied. "I was a doctor for many years before working for the museum."

Captain Nemo led me to the crew's quarters. Lying on the bed was a man with a terrible head wound.

"A collision broke one of the levers in the engine room,"

the captain explained. “It hit this man on the head.”

I examined him closely. “I’m afraid he will die within a few hours,” I said quietly.

I heard nothing more from Captain Nemo until the next morning, when he invited us to go on another excursion to the ocean bed. We put on our diving suits and stepped out onto the bottom of the sea. Here there was no fine sand like the bed of the Pacific Ocean. There was only coral, each bush more beautiful than the last.

Captain Nemo stopped and I noticed that his men were carrying something on their shoulders. At our feet, I noticed mounds of earth, each marked with a coral cross. The men raised their pickaxes and began to dig.

“This is a graveyard!” I thought.

Later, when the body was buried and we returned to the ship, I met Captain Nemo on the platform.

“Your dead sleep quietly there,” I said kindly, “beyond the reach of sharks.”

“Yes, Monsieur,” he replied sadly, “and beyond the reach of men.”

Chapter Six

Saving Captain Nemo

As we entered the Indian Ocean, I began to change my feelings about Captain Nemo. I no longer felt that he was a man to be pitied. After all, he had drugged us, imprisoned us and now a member of his crew had been wounded and killed. But I wanted to finish my underwater journey around the world with him. I wanted to see all the wonders of the water. I wanted to see things no man had seen before. However, we were coming close to land again – and I knew that Ned would want to escape. I would have to go with him.

"Let us wait until we are closer to Europe," I said to him. "Then we can decide what is the best thing to do."

By the end of January, we were approaching the coast of Ceylon, off the tip of southern India.

"Tomorrow, we shall visit the pearl fisheries," Captain Nemo said. "They are the best in the world, although the pearl fishermen are poorly paid for their work. By the way, Monsieur Aronnax, are you afraid of sharks?"

"I do not know much about them!" I replied.

"Perhaps we shall hunt them," he said. "It is an excellent sport."

I felt sweat trickle down my forehead. That night, I had nightmares full of sharks, their jaws glistening with sharp teeth. When I woke up at four o'clock, it was still dark outside and clouds covered the sky. The *Nautilus* had reached the famous pearl bed that stretched into the distance for more than twenty miles. We climbed into our dinghy as dawn broke, and the sun's rays pierced the clouds.

"In a month's time, when the pearls are ready, this water will be swarming with pearl divers," Captain Nemo explained. "Now let us put on our diving suits. We shall not be diving very deep so we can use the sunlight."

We set off. We all carried knives in our belts and Ned also carried an enormous harpoon. Once we were under the water, my fear vanished. As the sun grew stronger, I recognised oyster shells sparkling in the sand. An hour later, we reached the big oyster bed. Captain Nemo led us through it to the bottom of a circular pit. Then he stopped and pointed. In front of us was an oyster more than seven feet wide. The two halves of the shell were partly open. I leaned forward to look. The pearl inside was the size of a coconut.

As we wandered around the oyster bed, we saw a lone fisherman at work. He worked carefully and quickly until, suddenly, his face looked terrified. A giant shadow had appeared above him – the shadow of a shark. The monster's tail struck the man on the chest and threw him to the ocean floor. The animal turned, ready to bite the man in two.

I saw Captain Nemo walk towards the monster, dagger in hand. He plunged it into the shark's belly. It roared and the water turned red. Then he struck again and again as the

creature turned over and over. I was frozen with horror and could not go to help him. Captain Nemo fell to the ground and the shark came towards him, its jaws open wide.

Ned ran forward and struck the shark with his harpoon, reaching its heart. Captain Nemo pulled the fisherman to the surface and we all followed quickly. Then we made our way back to the dinghy.

"Thank you, Master Land," Captain Nemo said.

"You were full of kindness towards that fisherman," I said, "yet you are trying to avoid your fellow humans."

"That fellow is a poor man and I shall always support the

poor of this world," he replied.

"Where are you taking us, Captain Nemo?" I asked. "We have already travelled over sixteen thousand miles..."

"Seven and a half thousand leagues!" he interrupted.

"... and we are almost at the Persian Gulf," I continued. "How will we get to Europe?"

"I did not say we were heading for Europe," he replied. "Are you getting tired of this voyage under the sea?"

"Yes!" Ned cried. "Do you realise that we have been your prisoners for almost three months?"

"No, I did not," Captain Nemo said. "I am not counting."

"But when will it end?" Ned muttered. "One cannot be happy unless one is free."

Chapter Seven

The Arabian Tunnel

We sailed into the Red Sea as far as the newly built Suez Canal, which would have taken us straight into the Mediterranean Sea.

"It is too dangerous to go through a canal," Captain Nemo said. "But I promise you that we shall be in the Mediterranean Sea by tomorrow."

"You would have to travel at an astonishing speed to travel round the whole coast of Africa in one day," I said.

"Who said anything about going round the coast of Africa?" he replied.

"You're going to sail under it?" I asked, amazed.

"Why not?" the captain replied. "There is an underground passage in the rock all the way. I have named it the Arabian Tunnel. I have used it several times."

"How did you discover it?" I asked.

"It is simple," he replied. "I noticed that there were the same fish in the Red Sea and in the Mediterranean Sea. Since the Red Sea is higher than the Mediterranean, I realised that the sea current must have brought them. I put a copper ring around the tails of some fish in the Red Sea. A few months later, I caught them in the Mediterranean. So I looked for a tunnel in the rock and I found it."

A few hours later, as we approached the entrance to the tunnel, Captain Nemo invited me to the steering platform. We slowed down. Then the *Nautilus* plunged into the tunnel. I heard a strange rustling sound along its sides – the waters of the Red Sea roaring through a sloping tunnel towards the Mediterranean. We moved along as swiftly as an arrow. In less than twenty minutes, Captain Nemo turned towards me. "The Mediterranean Sea!" he said.

When Ned woke up the next morning and realised where we were, he spoke to me in private. "What I have to say is very simple, Professor. We are now in Europe. And before Captain Nemo drags us back to the depth of the sea, I suggest that we escape from the *Nautilus*."

My heart sank. "I don't want to leave," I thought. "Every day, I am learning more about the sea. I shall never have this chance again."

"I do not know what to do," I replied. "Common sense tells me that he will never let us go. And common sense tells me we should take the first chance we have to escape, but…"

"I warn you, I shall try to get the dinghy out if we are close to land," Ned interrupted.

"Remember, if the plan fails, we will all die," I said. "But I do not think we shall have the chance anyway. Captain Nemo will always be on his guard." I knew I had to decide. "Very well, Ned," I said at last. "When you are ready to escape, let us know and we will follow you."

Captain Nemo did not seem to trust us. The *Nautilus* remained under water almost all the time and we hardly saw him during our speedy crossing of the Mediterranean Sea. I estimated that we covered a distance of about fifteen hundred miles in forty-eight hours. Ned Land had to give up his idea of escape and he was very disappointed.

At last, we entered the Atlantic Ocean. There the *Nautilus* came to the surface and we were able to enjoy daily walks on the platform again although the sea was very rough. One evening, Ned followed me back to my cabin.

"It's all arranged," he said. "Nine o'clock tonight."

I looked at him in surprise. "But the sea is too rough, Ned," I replied.

"We must risk that," he said. "It is worth it to be free. In three hours we shall be on dry land – or dead!"

Chapter Eight

Atlantis

I stayed in my cabin, avoiding Captain Nemo in case he saw how worried I was. During these unhappy hours, I hoped that something would happen to make Ned change his mind. As the clock struck eight, I put on warm clothes and went to stand by the door that led to the staircase. I waited anxiously for Ned's signal.

Only the beating of my heart broke the silence. Suddenly, I noticed that the *Nautilus* had stopped. There was a slight bump as we settled on the ocean floor.

"We are too far from land to escape now," I thought. "Poor Ned!"

Just then the door of the saloon opened and Captain Nemo appeared. He called me to the window. There he pointed to his men outside in diving suits. They were clearing chests of silver and gold from a shipwreck.

"This money might have been given to the poor!" I protested.

"Do you think I am collecting this money for my benefit?" he replied angrily. "I still have pity for the poor. I shall give the money to them. I have done so many times."

Although Ned was furious with the delay, I felt as if a great weight had been lifted from my mind.

The next night, at about eleven o'clock, I received an unexpected visit from Captain Nemo.

"So far you have only explored the sea in daylight," he said. "Would you like to explore the ocean at night?"

"Yes, very much," I replied.

"I must warn you that this excursion will be very long and tiring," he said. "You will have to climb a mountain."

Nobody else came with us. At first, we walked through pitch-black water, sinking into a thick mud. The ground slowly rose, becoming rocky, and a whitish glow came from beyond the peak of a mountain. We walked towards that glimmer of light. It was wild and beautiful up there. We climbed above the tree line in two hours, shoals of fish rising from under our feet. The mountain side became rockier and full of crevices. Thousands of eyes sparkled in the darkness and claws closed with a snap. They belonged to giant lobsters and my blood froze every time I saw one.

At last, we reached a plateau. To my surprise, I saw a cluster of ruins – castles and temples – all draped with seaweed. Where was I? What part of the world had the sea swallowed up? I wanted to ask Captain Nemo, but he kept on walking and pointing to the top of the mountain.

At last we reached the peak, I looked across at a peak on the other side. It was a volcano, spewing out lava into the water around it, lighting up the valley with a brilliant glow.

Below me was the ruined city. Its roofs were sunken,

its temples demolished. There were the remains of a giant aqueduct, of an old port, crumbling walls and deserted streets – an ancient city buried beneath the sea. Captain Nemo picked up a chalky rock and scribbled one word: ATLANTIS.

I felt a thrill run through me. I had heard of this great city. Many historians believed that it existed and others did not. Now I was standing above it! I tried to fix all its details in my mind. We stood there for an hour, steeped in history, dreaming.

The rays of the moon pierced the waves and cast their

shadow on the city. It was only a dim light, but its effect was beautiful. Then we had to leave. We reached the *Nautilus* just as the first light of dawn was spreading its white glow on the surface of the sea.

We were now sailing a few yards below the Atlantic Ocean. Soon we entered a quiet area called the Sargasso Sea. Its calm surface, right in the middle of the Atlantic, was so thick with weeds that the Nautilus had to stay below the surface.

Ned Land was anxious. "Look at this vast sea!" he cried. "There are no islands. I shall never be able to escape."

"When this journey is over," I replied, "we shall try to persuade Captain Nemo to let us go. We shall promise never to give away his secrets."

It was now the middle of March and we were still travelling south. I expected to head west into the Pacific Ocean again as we passed the tip of South America. But we did not.

"I think we are heading for the South Pole," I said to Ned. "You were right to be worried. Nobody has ever gone there before." I paused.

"We shall be in great danger," I said at last.

Chapter Nine

The South Pole

Icebergs began to dot the sea. They were crowded with polar birds that deafened us with their cries. Some of them thought the *Nautilus* was a dead whale and tried to peck at its steel plates.

Captain Nemo did not speak at all as he steered us between the floating ice. He did it so well that I realised he must have been this way before. But, suddenly, on the 16th of March, our path was completely blocked by the ice fields. The *Nautilus* crashed through them at first, surrounded by thick fog and blown by violent winds. But two days later, we stopped. We were completely frozen in!

"We've come to the great ice shelf!" Ned cried. "Nobody has ever managed to travel through it."

"No," Captain Nemo replied, "but we can go under it."

We dived down and travelled for a whole day. At six o'clock the next morning, Captain Nemo knocked on the door of my cabin.

"Come and look, Professor," he said. "We've reached the open sea again! And beyond that, the South Pole!"

An hour later, we were standing on the island of Antarctica. Thousands of birds swooped in the air. Walruses and penguins lay over the rocks. As we walked, Captain

Nemo worked out exactly where we were. My heart was pounding with excitement as he spoke.

"The South Pole!" he shouted at last. He unrolled a black flag, with the letter N embroidered on it in gold, and fixed it into the ground.

When we returned to the *Nautilus*, the air tanks were filled and we dived to one thousand feet. At three o'clock in the morning, a violent shock woke me up and I felt the ship lean over. We all rushed up to speak to Captain Nemo. For the first time, his face was anxious.

"One of the icebergs has turned over," he explained. "It has struck us and has now slipped beneath the *Nautilus*. The iceberg is rising and taking us with it. If we strike the ice shelf, we shall be crushed."

We were now in a tunnel of ice about sixty feet wide, filled with calm water. We sailed on towards one end of the tunnel and found it blocked with ice. To our horror, the other end was blocked, too.

"Are we trapped, Captain Nemo?" I asked.

"Yes," he replied calmly. "There are two ways of dying, gentlemen. We can wait until the ice crushes us to death. Or we can suffocate through lack of air."

Captain Nemo decided that we must try to cut through the ice before our air ran out in two days' time. He landed the Nautilus on the iceberg below, where he found that the ice was thirty feet thick. We had to cut out a hole big enough for us to sail through. We put on diving suits and worked in shifts. But after twelve hours, we had dug out only three feet. And some of the water around us was beginning to freeze.

"It could crush us like glass!" I cried.

"We must stop the water outside from freezing," Captain Nemo muttered. He seemed lost in thought. At last, two words escaped from his lips: "Boiling water!"

Captain Nemo led me to the kitchens where huge machines boiled sea water to make it fit to drink. Hour after hour, he pumped this boiling water outside until the temperature began to rise, just enough to stop the water from freezing.

"We can only die from lack of air now," I thought.

By the next day, twenty feet of ice remained below us – two days' digging. The air inside the ship was very stale. We were half suffocated, dizzy and hardly able to breathe properly.

"We shall use the ship to crush the last of the ice," Captain Nemo announced.

We took on as much water as we could to increase the ship's weight. Then we began to sink towards the ice. I felt the *Nautilus* vibrate. The ice split open and we dropped through the hole. The pumps took the water out and we began to rise. But we were still under ice.

"How long before we reach the open sea?" I asked myself. "We shall all be dead by then."

I lay down. My lips were blue and I could no longer see or hear. Suddenly, I opened my eyes. I felt the *Nautilus* charge the ice above us. It broke though. The hatch was pulled open and waves of fresh air flooded the ship.

"Since we have been to the South Pole, do you think Captain Nemo would like to go to the North Pole next?" Ned asked.

Chapter Ten

Escaping the Whirlwind

We had been prisoners for six months and had travelled seventeen thousand leagues – over forty thousand miles – since we had left Japan. The *Nautilus* was now sailing off the coast of South America. As we came close to the Caribbean, Ned hoped that we could escape because there were so many islands. But Captain Nemo, realising this, kept well away from the coast. We sailed at a depth of about five thousand feet where we saw rocks carpeted with giant seaweed.

"This must be food for the giant squid that live in these waters," I said.

"Are they about twenty feet long?" Conseil asked, looking through the window. "And do they have eight tentacles and a horny beak like a parrot's?"

"That's right," I said. "How did you know?"

"Well, I'm looking at one right now!" he shouted.

I stared past him. This giant squid was twenty-five feet long and moving at great speed towards us. Other squid appeared at the window. I counted seven of them wriggling around the *Nautilus*, grinding their teeth against its metal. We came to a sudden stop.

"I imagine one of these creatures has wrapped itself around our propeller," Captain Nemo said. "We'll have to use axes."

"And my harpoon," Ned added.

We surfaced and began to open the hatch. A squid pulled off the top with its suckers and a tentacle slid through the opening. Captain Nemo cut it off with one blow of his axe and it slithered and squirmed down the steps. Two more tentacles snaked through the air and grabbed the man standing in front of Captain Nemo. We watched him dangling in the air, screaming and choking and shouting in French. I shall remember his screams for the rest of my life. We could not save him. As we cut off the tentacles one by one, the squid squirted a jet of black liquid, which blinded us for a few minutes. When we could see again, the squid had disappeared.

How angry we were as we fought the other squids! Ten or twelve of them now squirmed over the deck. We hurled ourselves against them, into a mass of blood and black ink. Ned threw his harpoon into one of the creature's eyes, but another squid knocked him over and opened its mouth wide over him. He was about to be bitten in half. I ran towards him, but Captain Nemo was quicker. He buried his axe in the squid's jaws and Ned leapt to his feet, throwing his harpoon into the monster's heart.

The battle lasted a quarter of an hour. Then the monsters, hacked and defeated, finally disappeared under the waves. Captain Nemo, spattered with blood, gazed into the sea that had just swallowed up one of his men, tears streaming down his cheeks.

We continued to sail north seven hundred feet below the sea. The Atlantic Ocean above us was full of ships sailing from New York to Europe.

"In a few days we shall be close to my home," Ned reminded me. "You must speak to Captain Nemo or I shall jump into the sea!"

I did as Ned asked. But Captain Nemo shook his head. "Monsieur Aronnax," he replied. "I will tell you today what I told you some months ago. Whoever enters the *Nautilus* must never leave her. Please do not speak to me about this again – ever."

A storm drove us north-east and we drifted through dangerous fogs until we came to Newfoundland. By the end of May, we had drifted close to the coast of Ireland. Would the *Nautilus* dare to enter the busy English Channel? On the first of June, we came to the surface to take in air. That's when we saw a ship sailing at full speed towards us, firing its guns.

"Of course!" I said to myself. "The *Abraham Lincoln* is still hunting the monster!" I remembered the night when we had been locked in our cells, the night the man had been injured. "That must have been an attack, too!" I thought.

"Go down below!" Captain Nemo roared with anger, his face pale. "I am going to sink her."

We had no choice but to obey him. But by the afternoon, I was so anxious that I could not bear waiting any longer. I decided to talk to Captain Nemo one last time. I begged him not to attack.

"Be silent!" he shouted. "It is because of men like those on that ship that I lost everything I loved – my wife, my children, my parents. I must take my revenge."

I did not reply. I returned instead to Ned and Conseil.

"We must try to reach the *Abraham Lincoln* as soon as she is near enough," I told them. "She will be sunk by dawn. It would be better for us to sink on board her than to be part of this act of revenge."

We waited all night. The *Abraham Lincoln* sailed so close that we got ready to make a dash for it. But suddenly, the *Nautilus* dived. I knew what this meant. She was going to ram the other ship from below. I felt the shock as we ploughed right through the ship. I ran from my cabin to the saloon. Captain Nemo was already watching through the window. The ship was sinking thirty feet away from me and its passengers writhed in the water. I stood there, unable to move, struck with horror as the panels closed over that terrible scene.

When it was all over, Captain Nemo, without a word, went to his cabin. I followed him angrily. I found him looking at a portrait of a young woman and two children. Then he fell to his knees and wept.

We sailed on for almost three weeks, zig-zagging across the Atlantic Ocean until we did not know where we were. We did not see any of the crew or Captain Nemo during this time. One day – I cannot say which it was because all the clocks had stopped – Ned woke me up at dawn.

"We are going to escape this evening!" he whispered. "I've just caught sight of land. We can't be more than twenty miles away. Will you come with me?"

I nodded. I had no doubts now.

"Come up to the dinghy at ten o'clock," he said.

The day seemed very long. When the time came, I crept through the dark corridors of the *Nautilus* to the saloon. I had to cross it to reach the staircase. To my horror, Captain Nemo was there, sitting in the darkness. I began to crawl along the carpet. Suddenly, he got up and came towards me, silent, his arms folded, gliding like a ghost across the floor. But he did not see me.

"Enough! Enough!" he cried, sobbing.

I climbed the staircase, went through the hatch and found Ned and Conseil waiting by the dinghy. We jumped inside and began to undo the screws that fastened it to the ship. Suddenly, we heard voices close by, repeating one word, one terrifying word: "Maelstrom! Maelstrom!"

"The whirlwind that blows off the coast of Norway!" I whispered. "No ship has ever escaped it. Perhaps that is why Captain Nemo has brought us here."

As we looked at one another in horror, the *Nautilus* began to spin round and round. We clung to each other, sick with terror.

"Tighten the screws again!" Ned shouted. "If we stay with the ship we may be saved!"

But it was too late. The screws were torn from their sockets. We were hurled into the middle of the whirlwind like a stone flung from a sling. My head struck the dinghy and I lost consciousness.

And so our voyage beneath the sea ended – a voyage of twenty thousand leagues. I do not know how we escaped the whirlwind. But Ned, Conseil and myself were thrown up onto some islands near the Norwegian coast.

What happened to the *Nautilus*? Is Captain Nemo still alive, lurking at the bottom of the sea? I do not know – but I hope so, and I hope that all the beauty he has seen shall one day take away his need for revenge.

Glossary

Key:

adj	adjective
adv	adverb
n	noun
phr	phrase
phr v	phrasal verb
(superl)	superlative
vi	intransitive verb
vt	transitive verb

aqueduct	*n*	a bridge that carries a canal, or a very large pipe filled with water, to supply water to a town	36
be on your (guard), to	*phr*	to be watching out for anything dangerous	33
belly	*n*	stomach	28
bow	*n*	the front of a boat or ship	9
bow and arrow	*phr*	an arrow is like a short spear; a	22
chart	*n*	a map of the sea	16
copper	*n*	a reddish-coloured metal	31
coral reef	*phr*	a mass of coral growing together; corals are very small sea animals that look like stone plants	21

course	*n*	the exact path that a ship travels	21
crevice	*n*	a large crack in a rock	35
crew	*n*	the people who work on a ship	9
deck	*n*	a floor or level of a ship; the open, top level of a ship	8
dinghy	*n*	a small boat	15
dot, to	*vt*	to be scattered about, here and there	38
extract, to	*vt*	to remove	14
fellow	*n*	a man	30
fellow humans	*phr*	other humans beings, like yourself	29
filter down, to	*phr*	if light filters down into a place, it comes into it but loses some of its brightness	19
glare	*n*	bright light that hurts your eyes	12
hacked	*adj*	badly cut	43
harpoon	*n*	a long stick with a sharp point and attached to a rope, used to kill whales	6
hatch	*n*	a small door in the deck of a ship	11
hull	*n*	the shell-like body of a boat	15
iceberg	*n*	a large mass of ice floating on the sea	38
jaws	*pl n*	the top and bottom parts of a mouth	21
lava	*n*	very hot, liquid rock	9

league	*n* *(old fashioned)*	a distance of about 5km or 3 miles	4
lever	*n*	part of a machine, like a stick that you move to work the machine	26
lurk, to	*vi*	if something lurks, it is present in a place and you feel threatened by it	5
maelstrom	*n*	(here) a violent wind that blows round and round; a whirlwind	47
mammal	*n*	mammals are animals that generally give birth to babies which drink milk from their mothers	7
mercy: at the mercy of…	*phr*	if you are at the mercy of something, you are in danger from it	22
outrun, to	*vt*	if you outrun another vehicle, you go faster than it	15
overboard	*adv*	if you go overboard, you fall into the water from a ship	22
peak	*n*	the top of a mountain	35
pickaxe	*n*	a large tool used for breaking rocks	26
plough through, to	*phr*	to break through the middle of something	45
propeller	*n*	the blades that turn in the water to make a ship move	10
prowl, to	*vi*	to move quietly, for example when hunting	22

quarters	*pl n*	the rooms or cabins where the crew live and sleep	25
ram, to	*vt*	to bang into	45
rudder	*n*	a long piece of metal or wood that goes down into the water and is used for steering	10
rustling	*n*	a gentle noise, like leaves in the wind	32
seethe, to	*vi*	to move violently in all directions	21
sling	*n*	a piece of cloth or leather used to throw stones	22
spew out, to	*phr*	if something spews out a substance, there is a lot of that substance flowing out	35
squid	*n*	a sea creature that has long tentacles	42
sucker	*n*	a cup-like structure on a tentacle that allows a creature to stick to things	43
suffocate, to	*vi*	if you are suffocating, you don't have enough air to breathe	10
support, to	*vt*	if you support a family, you earn money and pay for their needs (food, housing etc.)	4
swoop, to	*vi*	to drop through the air	38
take (your) bearings, to	*phr*	to work out your exact position	15

take (your) revenge, to	*phr*	to harm someone because they have harmed you	45
tentacle	*n*	a long, thin bit of flesh (an octopus, for example, has eight tentacles)	42
thrashing	*n*	violent movement	8
tree line	*phr*	the imaginary line on a mountain above which trees can't grow	35
walrus	*n*	a large, fat sea animal, similar to a seal, that has two very long teeth	38
whirlwind	*n*	a wind that blows round and round	47
widow	*n*	a woman whose husband has died	4
writhe, to	*vi*	to twist and turn violently	45
zig-zag, to	*vi*	to keep changing direction	46

20,000 Leagues under the Sea Test Yourself

Exercise 1

Choose the correct option.

1 Monsieur Aronnax's manservant was very CALM / WORRIED about the dangerous sea journey.

2 Ned Land was from FRANCE / CANADA.

3 Conseil was in the water with Aronnax because he was FLUNG OVERBOARD / DECIDED TO FOLLOW HIM.

4 Captain Nemo CAN / CANNOT speak French.

5 Nemo collided with the Abraham Lincoln because HIS SHIP'S STEERING WAS DAMAGED / HE WANTED TO DAMAGE THE ABRAHAM LINCOLN'S STEERING.

6 The Nautilus makes electricity from THE SODIUM IN SEAWATER / TANKS FULL OF AIR.

7 The Nautilus struck a coral reef in the TORRES STRAIT / FORESTS OF CRESPO.

8 Ned and Arronax were attacked by a group of Papuans with HARPOONS AND GUNS / BOWS AND ARROWS.

9 The Papuans couldn't enter the hatches because they were UNDERWATER / ELECTRIFIED.

10 One of Captain Nemo's crew was buried in the INDIAN OCEAN / PACIFIC OCEAN.

Exercise 2

Match the descriptions to the places the Nautilus visited.

1 This place is just off the southern tip of India.

2 Captain Nemo saved a fisherman here and Ned killed a shark.

3 They sailed from the Red Sea to the Mediterranean Sea through this.

4 Ned planned an escape from the Nautilus at nine o'clock in this sea.

5 A ruined city under the sea.

6 A quiet part of the Atlantic Ocean, thick with weeds.

7 A frozen land with penguins and walruses.

8 A place where giant squid live.

9 The Abraham Lincoln attacked the Nautilus again here.

10 A whirlwind blows in this place.

A Atlantis
B the Arabian Tunnel
C the Caribbean
D the Sargasso Sea
E the pearl fisheries
F the coast of Norway
G the English Channel
H the coast of Ceylon
I the island of Antarctica
J the Atlantic Ocean

Answers

Exercise 1

1 calm
2 Canada
3 decided to follow him
4 can
5 he wanted to damage the Abraham Lincoln's steering
6 the sodium in seawater
7 Torres Strait
8 bows and arrows
9 electrified
10 Indian Ocean

Exercise 2

1 h; 2 e; 3 b; 4 j; 5 a; 6 d; 7 i; 8 c; 9 g; 10 f